Little Red Riding Hood

Cover illustrated by
Angela Jarecki

Adapted by
Sarah Toast

Illustrated by
Susan Spellman

Copyright © 1996 Publications International, Ltd.
All rights reserved. This book may not be reproduced or quoted
in whole or in part by mimeograph or any other printed or electronic means,
or for presentation on radio, television, videotape, or film without permission from

Louis Weber, C.E.O.
Publications International, Ltd.
7373 North Cicero Avenue
Lincolnwood, Illinois 60646

Permission is never granted for commercial purposes.

Manufactured in U.S.A.

8 7 6 5 4 3 2 1

ISBN: 0-7853-1852-6

Publications International, Ltd.
Story Garden is a trademark of Publications International, Ltd.

There was once a little girl who lived in a small village at the edge of a very large forest. Everybody loved her.

Her grandmother, who lived in a house in the forest, loved the little girl most of all. The grandmother made her a beautiful red velvet riding cloak with a hood. The little girl wore it every day, everywhere she went, so she became known as Little Red Riding Hood.

Then one day Little Red Riding Hood's grandmother was feeling ill. Little Red Riding Hood's mother began to worry about the grandmother.

The morning after baking day, Little Red Riding Hood's mother said, "It would be very nice for Grandmother if you would take her some fresh bread and cakes." Little Red Riding Hood happily agreed and put on her hooded cloak.

"You must be very careful going through the woods by yourself," said her mother. "You must stay on the open path and walk quickly and quietly. Be careful not to stumble and drop the food you are carrying to Grandmother."

"I will be very careful," promised Little Red Riding Hood, and she started down the path through the woods to her grandmother's house.

It was not long before Little Red Riding Hood met a wolf on the path. She didn't know anything about hungry wolves, so she was not a bit afraid.

"Good morning," said the wolf. "Where are you going this fine day?"

"I'm going to my grandmother's little house under the three big oak trees," answered the girl. "I'm taking her a basket of good food to make her feel better."

The wolf thought that Little Red Riding Hood would make a tasty snack, but someone might come along the path any minute. So he slyly said he was going her way and asked if he could walk with her.

Little Red Riding Hood walked quickly along, as she had been told to do. The wolf, meanwhile, thought of a plan.

"Just look at those wildflowers at the side of the path!" he said. "Wouldn't it do your grandmother good to have a bouquet of pretty flowers?"

The girl looked around her and saw the sunlight dancing on the flowers. Surely it couldn't hurt to take just one step off the path to pick a flower for Grandmother! But one patch of flowers led to another, and soon Little Red Riding Hood had gone far from the path. She didn't notice that the wolf was no longer waiting for her.

The tricky wolf had gone on ahead to Grandmother's. Once there, he knocked on the door.

"Who's there?" called Grandmother.

The sly wolf answered in a high voice, "It is Little Red Riding Hood. I have brought you a basket of goodies!"

"Lift the latch, child," said Grandmother. "I cannot get out of bed."

The wolf lifted the latch, leaped in, and frightened Grandmother right out of bed. She ran to the cupboard and locked herself inside. The wolf then found a lacy cap and nightgown belonging to Grandmother and put them on. He climbed into her bed and pulled the covers up to his wolfy chin. Then he waited.

By now Little Red Riding Hood had picked a beautiful bouquet of flowers and found her way back to the path. She quickly walked the rest of the way to Grandmother's and knocked on the door.

"Who's there?" called the wolf, as he tried to make his voice sound old.

"It is I, Grandmother," said Little Red Riding Hood. "I have nice things for you."

"Lift the latch and come in," said the wolf.

So Little Red Riding Hood went in and wished her grandmother a good morning. She put the flowers in a jug and the food on the table.

Little Red went over to Grandmother's bedside. Grandmother looked so odd that Little Red Riding Hood felt frightened.

"Oh, Grandmother," she said. "What big ears you have!"

"The better to hear you with," said the wolf, in Grandmother's voice.

"And Grandmother, what big eyes you have," said Little Red Riding Hood.

"The better to see you with," said the wolf.

"But Grandmother, what big teeth you have," said Little Red Riding Hood.

"The better to eat you with!" cried the wolf in his own voice as he jumped out of bed.

As the wolf chased Little Red Riding Hood around and around the room, he tripped on the hem of the grandmother's long nightgown. Despite his clumsiness, the wolf just about trapped Little Red Riding Hood in a corner. But as good luck would have it, that was the corner where Grandmother was hiding in the cupboard.

At the right moment, Grandmother flung the cupboard door open with all her might and knocked the wolf off his feet. That gave Little Red Riding Hood a chance to run out the door and away from the house.

"Help! Help! The wolf is after me!" shouted Little Red Riding Hood.

As Little Red Riding Hood ran down the path crying for help, a hunter heard her calls. He had been tracking this mischievous wolf for days and had noticed the paw prints on the path leading to Grandmother's house.

As the angry wolf dashed out of the house after Little Red Riding Hood, the hunter took aim with his rifle. He fired one shot, and the wolf fell dead.

At that, Little Red Riding Hood turned right around and ran back into the house to look for her grandmother. Inside, she found her leaning shakily against the cupboard.

Grandmother and Little Red Riding Hood invited the hunter in to thank him. They sat down to enjoy some baked goodies, and soon Grandmother felt much better.

As the kind hunter walked Little Red Riding Hood home, she said to herself that she would never go off the path again.